The first Adv
Bobby the Robin

Malcolm Fearnside

MAPLE
PUBLISHERS

The First Adventure of Bobby the Robin

Author: Malcolm Fearnside

Copyright © Malcolm Fearnside (2022)

The right of Malcolm Fearnside to be identified as author of this work has been asserted by the author in accordance with section 77 and 78 of the Copyright, Designs and Patents Act 1988.

First Published in 2022

ISBN 978-1-915492-48-7 (Paperback)

Book Cover Design, Illustrations and Layout by:
White Magic Studios
www.whitemagicstudios.co.uk

Published by:
Maple Publishers
1 Brunel Way,
Slough,
SL1 1FQ, UK
www.maplepublishers.com

Index

Characters in order of appearance

Bobby the Robin and main character

Tiger – An Orange tabby cat

Black dog – A Dobermann.

Food

Stripey seeds – Are sunflower seeds.

Soft white stuff with seeds – A fat block.

Brown 'hairy' looking insects[1] – Are Dried meal worms.

Small round seeds – Are Millet seeds.

---

1 Bobby is confused. They look a bit like Wire worms, which Bobby knows. Bobby has never seen a dried meal worm.

Chapter 1

Go

This was Bobby's first adventure. He did not think of it as one, and it was one he did not want to have. He was nervously and sadly going along the edge of the hedgerow, along a quiet country lane. He was called Bobby because of his habit, when he could, of bobbing along the ground. In his short life he had discovered that if he bobbed along the ground he would see more insects and seeds to eat. Unlike, if and when he flew somewhere, and looked round for food.

He was nervous and sad because he was now considered an adult Robin. In Robin law you were not allowed to remain at home as an adult. His daddy had told him he had to leave home and find his own way in the big wide world. He had to find his own place, establish his own territory, and defend it against other male Robins.

Bobby is told to leave

That was just the way it was and had always been, and he was now on his own. His daddy said "I have taught you everything you need to know, so it is up to you, and good luck." Silently saying to himself "You will need it," as he remembered his own coming of age experience.

Bobby carried on bobbing along the bottom edge of the hedgerow for a long time, when he started to feel hungry. He had been keeping one eye out for danger and the other for food. However it was just before Christmas and all the insects seem to have disappeared. He had been looking at the grasses, but all the seeds had gone, and he had not seen any berries left in the hedgerow either. He continued bobbing along the lane getting hungrier and hungrier.

He could not help thinking back to the days when his mum and dad always did everything for him.

Bobby looking for a new home

Even recently when he had not found any food they always had some to give him. He had to eat to survive and was getting hungrier and hungrier. It was December, the ground was white and very cold. Not that he knew it was December, just it was very cold.

White and very cold

Chapter 2

Mobbed

Carrying on bobbing along feeling more and more despondent, he spotted a path on the right. He could not see where it went, but it was clear of snow, so looked encouraging. It turned a corner and opened up into a large cleared area. This was good, because he knew that people would have had to have done this. People usually, his daddy had told him, meant there was a good chance of food. Peering here and there, and over and under everything, he was disappointed not to find any food.

When suddenly it went dark, and he was surrounded by a huge mob of hundreds of speckled breasted birds, with long sharp pointed yellow beaks.

"This was serious" thought Bobby as he was being pecked by those sharp yellow beaks. "Stop it", shouted Bobby. It stopped when one of them swaggered up to him. Demanding to know who he was? What was he doing here?

Bobby is surrounded

"I am Bobby the Robin and I was just looking for place to live", replied Bobby. "You are lying. This is our place. You were spying. Who are you spying for?" Demanded the leader. "Saw you looking the place over. Looking into corners and everywhere" said the leader. "I am not a spy. I am not spying for anyone. I was just looking for some food" explained Bobby. "I will be on my way, and won't bother you any more" said Bobby.

"Oh! No you won't, you will stay here until we decide what to do with you" said the leader whilst turning to his flock and saying "So now we know the real reason why he was here. He was trying to find our food to steal" "Ouch, ouch" screamed Bobby as the nearest pecked him again. "We take a very serious view of thieves here. Severe cases are dealt with a thousand pecks" the leader said.

All of a sudden they flew off into a swooping, soaring murmuration[1]. He did not care why, he was free and flew quickly away.

---

1   That is what a large group of formation flying Starlings is called.

A Murmuration

Chapter 3

Disappointment and Truth

He hid under the hedge by the road and straightened out his feathers. Then hugging the hedge Bobby continued bobbing along the lane. He could fly, but did not know which direction to go, and he could miss seeing some food to eat. He had now gone further than he had ever been with his parents, and that was a little frightening. He did not know what he might come across. Was there a reason his parents had not gone any further?

He thought he was now far enough away to be able to start looking for a place where he could make his own home. There was however a big problem. There was no food anywhere that he could see. If he built a house here, where would he go for a continuing supply of food?

No! He would have to continue going further. He made two small detours to explore some possible trees. One had a very large nest in it, so Bobby made a quick retreat.

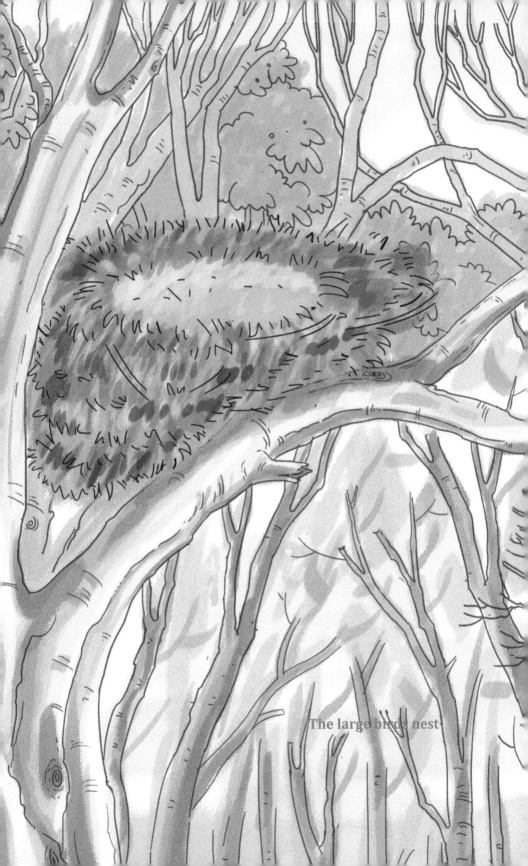

The large birds' nest

Now was not the time to have a very large unknown neighbour. The other? The continuing problem of no visible source of food.

Bobby was now getting very hungry, and it was past midday. He had not imagined it would be this difficult to find a place. The innocence of youth. He thought I will just go a little way, find a suitable place, and build my nest next to a reliable source of food.

After all his parents had done it, how difficult could it be? He was finding out how difficult it was to set up your own home.

He thought he knew all that was needed, but was finding he was completely unprepared. He was always going to ask his parents the important questions tomorrow. Like. How did you decide to make your home in this area? How did you decide what was a good tree? How did you decide that was to be the shape of your home? He now knew that tomorrow was too late.

Nothing to eat

Chapter 4

At Last a House

At long last he saw a big house in the distance. He remembered that sometimes when he went with his parents, they had taken him to one of these houses. They said you can usually find food at these places. He started feeling optimistic and hurried along the hedgerow, BUT, he had had to go into the open to cross the road, and was very nervous after what had happened to him.

He peered through the hedge and saw that there was a small table with some food on it. There was also a big glass window with more food on the ledge in front of the window. Through the window he could see lots of small pictures of himself on cards on the walls.

Oh! He was so happy the people who lived here loved Robins, there were pictures of him everywhere. He thought to himself "I have found my territory, but first I have to eat and then make a place to live."

At last a house

He was about to make a bee-line to the table with the food, when a big striped Orange cat came into view. He was prowling towards the food table. His dad had warned him about cats, they were dangerous, and to stay well clear of them.

He could fly there, but the table and window ledge seemed a bit low. He was not sure he would be safe, and the cat could catch him. Oh! What to do. I could fluff up all my feathers and make myself twice as big, but I would still be too small. I could wait until Tiger went away, but how long would that be? He was feeling really, really hungry now, and this was the only food he had seen all day. The day was fast disappearing and this seemed his only opportunity to eat. Looking around to see if there was any other food, he saw a dog asleep in his house.

His dad had told him dogs were not usually a problem as they left birds alone.

Bobby's afraid of Tiger

If they did get interested, they were too slow, so were not a problem. This was going to be tricky. The day was nearly over. This was the first food he had seen, and he did not want to go elsewhere.

He knew he could fly really fast, but did not know how fast Tiger was. There was a possibility that if Tiger was near the table he could fly to the window and grab some seeds quickly, and get away before Tiger could react. He needed more than just a beak full, so would have to chance darting back and forth from the window, to the table and so on. That idea seemed too risky. Oh! What to do?

Chapter 5

Brave Bobby

He remembered, once when he had gone with his daddy to get food they had seen a dog chasing a cat. That gave him an idea. What if he could wake up the dog? Perhaps it would chase the cat away and he could get to the food.

Bravely he flew on to the top of the dog's house. He thought that Tiger would not get him there. Though he could see Tiger was interested and was creeping closer. It had to be now. He flew quickly down, and gave Black dog a peck on his big black nose. Quick as a flash he flew back on top of black dog's house.

Tiger had jumped at Bobby but was not quick enough. Black dog gave a yelp. The first thing he saw was Tiger. Just in front of him. He could not believe Tiger was brave enough to scratch him on his nose. He had to be taught a lesson.

So with a great bark he leapt out of his house. Tiger had been so intent on Bobby he was nearly not quick enough to get away. With a shriek he turned and ran for his life.

Bobby was so pleased his plan had worked, he forgot for a moment why he was here. He bobbed and bobbed to-an-fro, and up and down with delight. All that bobbing had used up more energy and reminded him he needed to eat.

He flew onto the table of food and started to eat as fast as he could. All the time nervously looking round to make sure it was still safe. There was such a selection of food he did not recognise. Should he carry on eating the small round seeds or try some of the unknowns. There were bigger, different colour, round seeds, long ones, some stripey ones, some soft white stuff with seeds in it, and some long brown looking sort of insects.

Tiger runs for his life

They did not wriggle or move, so he was not sure they were insects. If only his mum or dad were here, they would tell him.

He did not know it made no difference which ones he chose, as Robins and other birds cannot taste any difference, they just go by shape and colour. He did not know that when he was growing up his parents were feeding all these things to him. He just waited with his beak wide open until his parents returned and put food in his mouth. He never saw what it was. All that mattered was he could eat it, and it gave him energy.

Bobby celebrates

Which ones were best he would have to work out for himself, by experience? So now was not the time for experiments that would come later. Now was the time to eat what he knew, so he carried on eating the small round ones. Though he kept looking at those strange, 'hairy' looking sort of insects.

Time to eat

Chapter 6

Shelter and safety

Having filled himself up with food he thought he had better find himself a place to spend the night. There was not time to make a permanent place of his own, so he would have to find a temporary one for the night.

It had to be out of reach of Tiger. Out of this cold weather and it was important to have a quick means of escape. Looking around he saw next to the big house was a small house made of wood that had a hole near the top. That looked promising, so he flew to the hole and looked in.

He saw that it was full of rows and rows of short round orange looking things, that could become nests but they were all full of earth except one. One seemed full of dead dry grass that could be used. Pushing grass here and there and with a bit of knowledge of watching his parents repairing his last nest. Those round orange pots were good nests with the right insides. Pity it was just temporary.

Bobby's temporary home

He saw that he had at last managed to make an acceptable bed for the night and settled down. He looked round and felt safe, he had that hole to escape if necessary, and was out of the weather, and what was more he was full. Thinking back over his day, had given him the shivers. Those birds, felt now like a nightmare, but his feathers showed it had been all too real. It would not do any good to think in the past, he had to plan for the future.

Bobby in his temporary home

Chapter 7

The Plan

He started to dream of what his new home would look like, but this would not do. He was getting too far ahead of himself. First he had to come up with a plan. He did not want to waste time tomorrow morning thinking what to do. He was O.K. for now, but could not stay here for a long time. It looked like this place was used by people from the big house. I have found a place with a source of food that is one problem solved[1].

Next. Where? Have to see if I can make friends with some other birds, who can point me in the right direction. Would there be a problem in setting up home here? Were there others of his kind already living here? That would ruin all his plans. He did not really want to have to fight to claim this territory. It also meant he would have to win. If I can stay here, I need to find building materials.

---

1   There are three needs for survival. 1. Food. 2. Shelter. 3. Warmth.

I know what my parents nest looked like. I imagine that design has passed the test of time and been handed down to each generation. I don't think it would be a good idea to try and create a new design.

I will need a good supply of twigs of all different sizes. Long twigs for the foundation.

Thinner more flexible ones for the walls. His Dad's nest did not have a roof, as the big branch above kept the rain out. That meant finding a suitable tree. If not, he would have to build a roof. How does one go about building a roof? How do you fix it in position? What would it be made out of? He had absolutely no idea. I do hope I can find a suitable tree.

I will next need to line the walls with something to keep out the wind. Something to make a carpet from, and also a bed. All these things in order to make his home comfortable.

He relaxed, and felt he had come up with a good plan of action for tomorrow. As he relaxed the day started to catch up with him, and he started feeling sleepy.

After all it had been quite a first day in the rest of his life. He was sure he would have many more interesting days to come. As he starting to feel a little bit pleased with himself he drifted off fast asleep.

Authors Note

Bobby's story was inspired by three things:-

1. Bobby was a soft fluffy toy that my late wife bought. When our Grand-children stayed, we used to make up stories about the Robin, who became real in our dreams, we called him Bobby.

2. Seeing a Robin fly out of our shed, which had a hole at the top, I looked in and found the Robin had built a nest in one of our many orange plastic flower pots, one of which had a dead plant in it. It was used until late spring, when one day the Robin was gone and never came back. That gave me the idea of it being a temporary home.

3. The interaction of the birds, came as a result of watching the birds feed at our feeding station just outside our kitchen window. The Blue tits and the Robin's feed quite happily alongside one another. The Sparrow's however come in numbers and frighten all the other birds away, except the Blue tits. They just look up, ignore them, and carry-on feeding. Twenty five years have passed and our Great-grand children are now at a similar age. I have forgotten most of the stories I made up, so this time I have decided to write them down. Perhaps the Great-great grand children will someday read them, and enjoy them as much as their Grand-parents did.

Prologue

The Second Adventure of Bobby the Robin - A New Dawn

Chapter 1
Making Friends

Bobby wakes up, with a start, something was wrong. Where was everyone? Then as he became wide awake he realised nothing was wrong, there was no one else, he was on his own. Settling down, he stretched his wings and hopped out of his nest. Flying up to the hole he poked his head out to check if it was all clear. It was. Looking at the food on the table he saw a number of other birds all eating together. That was a good sign, so he flew down to the food and said "Hello," No one took any notice of him, so he just started eating.

He noticed the Yellow vests were eating the stripey seeds. The Black caps were tucking into the soft white stuff with seeds in it. That left the small round seeds for him to eat again. Bobby was eating the small round seeds, when the nearest Yellow vest spoke to him. "Hello! Sorry I did not reply when you said Hello. I had my mouth full. Have not seen you here before." "No. I only arrived late yesterday." "Come far have you?" "It seemed like a long way," Bobby said.

"He then told his new friend that he had been told to leave his home by his parents." "That's awful. We all live together in the same neighbourhood. Why?" asked Yellow vest. Bobby explained that it was according to Robin law. When you became an adult you had to leave and find your own home. It had to be in a different area to the one you live in, and where there were no other Robin's, as you would be attacked. "Have you seen any of my kind here?" asked Bobby. "No. You are the first, so you not have to worry about that.........

Upcoming Books in the Series

- The Second Adventure of Bobby the Robin – A New Dawn
- Bobby the Robin's Third Adventure – The Trials of Work
- Bobby the Robin's Fourth Adventure – Home in Ducs' Wood
- Bobby the Robin's Fifth Adventure – Life and Death in Ducs' Wood
- Bobby the Robin's Sixth Adventure – Bobby Springs into action
- Bobby the Robin's Seventh Adventure – Kidnap and War

Lightning Source UK Ltd.
Milton Keynes UK
UKHW021558011222
413107UK00008B/91

9 781915 492487